D1454985

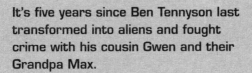

It's five years since Ben Tennyson last transformed into aliens and fought crime with his cousin Gwen and their Grandpa Max.

Now 15 years old, Ben is once again forced to turn to the Omnitrix to help fight a new and more sinister threat – the HighBreed, DNAliens and the Forever Knights, who team up to take over the world.

The watch-like Omnitrix has re-programmed itself and has a complete set of ten, brand new alien choices for Ben to get to grips with. Helped by his cousin Gwen with her magical powers and Ben's former enemy, Kevin E. Levin, Ben is soon all set to go hero once again!

NOW READ ON . . .

EGMONT

We bring stories to life

This edition first published in Great Britain 2010
by Egmont UK Limited
239 Kensington High Street
London W8 6SA

Cartoon Network, the logo, Ben 10 ALIEN FORCE
and all related characters and elements are trademarks
of and © 2010 Cartoon Network

Adapted by Barry Hutchison

1 3 5 7 9 10 8 6 4 2

Printed and bound in Great Britain

The Forest Stewardship Council (FSC) is an international,
non-governmental organisation dedicated to promoting
responsible management of the world's forests. FSC operates
a system of forest certification and product labelling that
allows consumers to identify wood and wood-based products
from well-managed forests.

For more information about Egmont's paper buying policy,
please visit www.egmont.co.uk/ethicalpublishing
For more information about the FSC, please visit their
website at www.fsc.org

PARADOX

CHAPTER ONE

THE ARMY BASE

In a top secret military base, a grey-haired army general was getting nervous. He was standing inside the observation booth of a laboratory, watching his two best scientists put the finishing touches to an experiment that could change the world. If everything went to plan then today – November 12th, 1955 – would go down in history.

If everything went according to plan. But the general's gut instinct told him something was going to go wrong, and those instincts had never failed him before.

He picked up the handset of the telephone he used to communicate with the main lab and barked into it. 'Sure this thing is gonna work?

Your time machine has cost the US government a pretty penny, doctor.'

The doctor leading the experiment gestured towards an enormous circle of stone and metal. It was mounted on a raised platform and filled most of the lab. Hundreds of wires and cables connected it to a control terminal.

'The Chronologger is hardly a time machine in the sense of a vehicle,' the scientist explained, 'but rather a subatomic drill designed to bore a tunnel in the fabric of space–time.' He turned to the glass screen, behind which the general was standing. 'As to cost, I would say that the alleviation of untold human suffering throughout history is ample justification.'

'It'll also give our enemies overseas a thing or two to think about,' the army commander grunted.

'But to answer your first question,' smiled the doctor, 'there is only one way to find out.'

On cue, everyone in the lab, including the

doctor and the general, pulled a pair of thick protective goggles over their eyes. Once he was sure everyone was covered up, the doctor crossed to the control terminal and pulled the activation lever.

SWOOOOOSH!

Almost at once, the huge contraption began to shudder and shake. A wind whipped up from inside the ring, sending notes and books hurtling across the lab.

'You're certain we're safe, doctor?' asked his assistant. He was standing a little further from the machine, monitoring the bank of energy readings.

'I'm not certain of anything, Hugo,' the doctor admitted. 'But the chrono-magnetic field we've created should protect us.'

Hugo wasn't convinced. 'Doctor,' he began, 'I . . . I'm frightened.'

The doctor rummaged in his pocket and pulled out a bag of sweets. 'Have a gumball,' he said, offering the bag to Hugo. 'It'll help calm your nerves.'

Suddenly, lights began to flash across the surface of the Chronologger. The howling wind became even more fierce. It swirled into a tornado and tore through the lab.

Hugo watched, helplessly, as the contents of the lab began shuddering across the floor towards the machine. He cried out in shock as a cabinet flipped into the air. It flipped end over end a few times, before being sucked into the time machine.

All around him, desks, chairs and bits of machinery were being pulled into the middle of the stone circle. Each one seemed to stretch out like rubber, then vanish through the hole in the heart of the machine.

Hugo glanced down at the energy readings. They were off the scale. He had to warn the doctor. The experiment had to be stopped!

Before Hugo could say a word, the doctor began to slip. He swung his arms, trying to retreat backwards, but it was too late. His body became elastic, and with a strangled scream he was swallowed by the Chronologger.

A second later, a large shadow passed across the lab, and something the world had never seen before let out a deep, terrifying roar.

Kevin's car cruised along a narrow desert road, throwing up clouds of sand in its wake. The sun was beating down, making the three occupants of the vehicle hot and irritable.

'You didn't need to come,' Kevin muttered. 'Gwen and I could have handled this alone. It's nothing, really.'

'It doesn't sound like nothing,' said Ben from the back seat, as Kevin pulled the car over. 'Weird noises. Unearthly lights. Rumours of weird creatures out here.'

They threw open their doors and all three of them stepped out on to the dusty road. Before them stood the thick, imposing walls of a long-abandoned army base.

'Yeah, the dudes I heard it from aren't totally reliable,' Kevin admitted.

'Isn't that like a big bad boy thing to do?' asked Gwen with a smirk. 'Come out here to the ghost town to drag race?'

'How should I know? I just know them

from the auto shop,' Kevin claimed.

'Grandpa Max said Las Solardad used to be a big military base back in the fifties,' said Ben. 'Some kind of research facility.'

Kevin nodded. 'Yeah. Must've been some pretty serious research. Check out these walls. Fifty years later and there's still no way in.'

Gwen gave a little cough. She had wandered away a little, and was standing beside two giant holes in the wall.

'No way,' Kevin frowned. 'They definitely didn't tell me about these.'

Gwen and Ben walked through one of the holes, while Kevin steered the car through another. Once they were all inside the base, Kevin got out of the car to join the others.

The base was laid out like a small town. Dozens of buildings lined a network of cracked, crumbling roads. Every one of the buildings was little more than a boarded-up ruin, long since abandoned.

From inside, it was possible to make out a few more holes in the walls of the base.

'Has anyone noticed that some of them are vaguely person-shaped?' asked Gwen.

Ben looked around at the holes. 'Weird,' he said. 'Maybe something, I don't know, burned through the wall.'

'Like what?' asked Kevin.

Ben pointed down to the ground, where a deep track had been carved through the tarmac surface of the road. 'The same thing that burned these weird trails everywhere.'

Gwen crouched down, examining something on the desert floor. 'Look,' she said.

Ben followed her gaze and soon spotted a tiny, perfectly-formed skeleton. 'This is a bird,' he said. Something at his feet caught his eye. He bent and carefully picked it up. 'And these are lizard bones. They're fossilised.'

Gwen straightened up. 'And they're not the only thing.'

One of the trenches in the ground led to an old telephone box. The box itself was a tangle of rusted metal, and two deep footprints were scorched into the stone floor, inside the telephone box.

'It's like someone turned the stone into dust just by standing on it,' said Gwen.

Kevin smirked. 'He was probably put on hold.'

Ben's eyes followed the route of the trench in the ground. 'The trail goes to the police station,' he announced. 'Then to those . . . I guess they're apartments.'

'So,' began Kevin, 'going by those fossils, someone stood here a million years ago and walked to those buildings that were built about fifty years ago?'

'You are not helping,' Ben sighed. 'These could be signs of serious DNAlien activity, and it's up to us – '

'DNAliens are not doing this,' said Gwen,

cutting him off. She raised a hand and pointed to where a weird, glowing-blue creature was snaking across the base. 'Does that look like a DNAlien to you?'

Ben had to admit that it didn't look like a DNAlien, but it did look dangerous. And he knew just how to deal with danger. The Omnitrix bleeped into life as he twisted the control dial.

It was butt-kicking time!

CHAPTER TWO

GROW UP, KEVIN

Kevin kept his eyes locked on the strange creature while he knelt down and pressed his fingers against the road, absorbing its energy. 'Finally,' he grinned, as his body began to turn to living concrete, 'something worth the trip.'

Gwen tensed, her fingertips glowing

with power. Beside her, Ben slammed his hand down on the Omnitrix. A swirl of green energy wrapped around him. When it cleared, his alien form towered above his two companions.

'ChromaStone!' he cried, as the transformation into his indestructible alien form was completed.

And not a second too soon. The blue, snake-like creature swerved around the group and brushed against the side of one of the crumbling old buildings.

KEREEEAK!

The area that the thing had touched

disintegrated into dust, and the whole building suddenly leaned sideways. ChromaStone looked up in time to see the entire structure toppling towards them.

'Look out,' he cried. He threw himself at Gwen and Kevin, wrapping his arms around them and dragging them out of harm's way.

CRAASH!

The building came down in a cloud of sand and sawdust. Sharp shards of the slate roof rained to the ground, missing the heroes by just millimetres.

ChromaStone leapt to his feet and spun in the direction the creature had gone. Another trench in the ground was the only sign that it had ever been there.

'Gone,' muttered the alien. In a flash of bright green he morphed back into Ben.

Gwen stood up and dusted herself down. 'Well, at least the building it destroyed wasn't the library.'

'You really like the books,' said Kevin, also transforming back into his normal form.

Ben sighed. 'She's saying we have to research. Find out what that thing is.' His eyes followed the criss-crossed tracks on the ground. 'All we know so far is that it's looking for something here on the base.'

Twenty minutes later, Gwen was sitting in front of an old-fashioned monitor, studying old microfilms of the base's research documents. It hadn't taken them long to find the library, but finding the information they needed was proving more difficult.

'These films are really corroded,' she complained, scrolling through another few pages of the documents. 'But it looks like this base was built for some kind of time experiment called "Project Paradox".'

Standing behind her, Kevin frowned. 'Who wouldn't pick the desert outside Bellwood to do top-secret research?'

'They built it here because of the huge quartz deposits,' Ben explained, reading from the screen.

Leaning over his cousin's shoulder, Ben studied the photograph of a man on the screen.

'His name's been censored,' said Ben. 'Whoever he was, his paradox theory was the basis of some kind of experimental tunnel through time.'

Ben straightened up. If there were scientists carrying out research on the base, then that meant only one thing. Somewhere nearby there had to be a lab.

The laboratory was in even worse condition than the rest of the base. Moss grew over the stone walls and ceiling. The glass screen of the observation booth was cracked and broken. A deep trench ran the whole length of the floor, right up to the strange, circular object that stood on a raised platform at the far end of the lab.

'Looks like my place after that big party I threw last weekend,' observed Kevin.

Gwen pointed down at the groove carved into the stone floor. 'Look, that thing's been here, too.'

'Only one trail,' said Ben. 'It either came in here and vanished – '

'Or it was born here,' concluded Gwen.

A sound from behind startled them. Moving on instinct, Kevin absorbed the properties of the concrete floor. Ben's hand flew to the Omnitrix and pushed down the dial.

'Swampfire!' he roared, as he

transformed into another of his alien forms. In a heartbeat he was through the door of the observation booth.

Something moved in the half-darkness. Pouncing, the alien caught hold of the shape and dragged it into the light.

'Gotcha!' he cried.

The face of the man they'd seen in the photograph gazed up at Swampfire. The doctor smiled warmly, and as he did his eyes twinkled with friendly mischief.

'Swampfire. That takes me back,' he said, before his eyebrows folded into a frown. 'Or is it forward? It's so hard to tell, Ben. In fact, have we met?'

'How do you know my name?' demanded Swampfire, releasing his grip on the man's white lab coat.

'Have we met yet, I suppose the question was,' continued the scientist.

'Hey,' said Kevin. 'It's that dork from the

photo. The paradox guy.'

'You haven't changed at all,' Gwen gasped. 'In fifty years.'

The doctor rummaged in his pocket and pulled out a crumpled paper bag. 'Oh, considerably more than that,' he smirked. 'Gumball?'

'No thanks,' said Swampfire, pushing the outstretched bag away. 'Who are you? What's your name?'

'You just read my file,' shrugged the doctor. 'I was rather hoping you could tell me. It slipped my mind several hundred years ago.'

'Did he just say "several hundred years"?' asked Kevin.

'Did you just say . . .' began Swampfire, before realising the man had vanished.

'By the way,' called a voice from behind them. The three heroes turned to find the doctor standing across the room. 'You didn't happen to see a space–time anomaly around here, did you?' He held up his hand to just above the level of his shoulder. 'About this big? Incredibly destructive, virtually unstoppable.'

The doctor waited for a reply, but none came. 'No? I must have been thinking of another moment,' he said with a shrug. 'Ta-ta.'

Turning on his heels, the doctor stepped through the door and left the lab. Kevin hurried after him, then stopped in the empty corridor.

'Where'd he go?'

Gwen pointed out of the window. The doctor was across the street, leaning casually on a rusted old street light. 'He's out there,' said Gwen.

'He's obviously connected to that creature,' said Swampfire. 'We really need to talk to him.'

'Oh yeah,' growled Kevin, cracking his concrete knuckles. 'We'll talk.'

With a roar, Kevin smashed a hole through the wall of the lab. His stone feet thudded on the ground as he charged, fists raised, towards the scientist.

But with a wink and a nod of his head, the doctor stepped behind the narrow lamppost. And disappeared!

Kevin skidded to a stop, unable to believe what he'd just seen. 'Huh?'

From across another street, Kevin heard the sound of someone clearing their throat. The doctor stood in a doorway, waving happily. He stepped inside the building and closed the door as Kevin charged towards him.

KARAAACK!

The old wooden door shattered to splinters as concrete Kevin hurtled through it. Outside, Swampfire and Gwen watched the old building shake and tremble. Kevin was tearing it to pieces, searching for the doctor.

A footstep scuffed on the pavement behind them. 'Was I in there?' the doctor asked. Grinning, he turned and ran around the outside of another building.

Swampfire and Gwen were quickly joined by Kevin. They blasted through the building, hoping to cut the doctor off before he could make it all the way round.

And when they emerged on the other side of the boarded-up house, the man was nowhere to be seen. They turned to find him standing behind them, leaning casually against the wall they had just destroyed.

'That was public property, you know?'

Swampfire shook his head. 'How does he move so fast?'

A voice from a little to their right surprised them. 'You mean how do I move so quickly?' corrected the doctor. He was across yet another street, even though none of them had even seen him move. 'It's called "walking",' he explained. 'Strolling, really.'

Kevin charged again, but this time the scientist didn't move. Kevin grabbed him by the lapels of his lab coat.

'Easy on the jacket, it's twelve hundred years old.' A twinkle danced behind the doctor's eyes. 'Anyway, thanks.'

'Thanks?' frowned Swampfire.

'For what exactly?'

'Well, I had a feeling if we made a loud enough racket he'd show up.' The doctor nodded along the street. The blue, snake-like creature was zig-zagging towards them.

'Finally,' growled Kevin, releasing his grip on the doctor. 'Something we can fight.'

'Oh, I really don't think that's a good idea,' the doctor warned, but it was too late. Kevin was already thundering towards the creature, his concrete hands clenched into fists.

'Those trails,' said Gwen, suddenly

figuring everything out. 'They're not trail marks, they're age. The creature accelerates time.'

The doctor nodded. 'Very good.'

Kevin caught up with the weird blue snake and swung with a devastating punch.

The creature didn't even seem to notice the blow, which passed harmlessly through its glowing blue surface. Kevin, on the other hand, couldn't help but notice. The moment his fist made contact, his concrete shell vanished. Kevin let out a cry of shock as an agonising pain gripped his whole body. The others could only watch as he collapsed on to the road.

The doctor set off in pursuit of the creature, leaving Swampfire and Gwen to tend to their fallen friend. They both recoiled in horror when they rolled him on to his back.

Kevin's skin was as wrinkled as a dried up leaf. His normally jet-black hair was wispy and grey, with a wide bald-spot on top of his head. Even his teeth had rotted away to nasty blunt yellow stumps.

It had taken only a few seconds, but somehow, just by touching the creature, Kevin had aged over eighty years!

CHAPTER THREE

RACE AGAINST TIME

Ben – now back in his human form – took hold of one of Kevin's arms, while Gwen took the other. Together they hauled him to his feet. 'We must get him to a hospital,' said Ben.

Suddenly, Kevin gave a cough and sprang into life. He pulled away from the cousins and raised his fists. 'What're you doing?' he wheezed. 'Get your hands off me.'

'Come on, Kevin,' pleaded Gwen. 'We're gonna get you some help.'

'What do you mean, "help"?' Kevin grimaced. 'I'm gonna kick that thing!' He swung a leg to demonstrate, then yelped as his hip made a loud cracking sound. 'Ow!' he spluttered, clutching his aching joints.

'Are you OK?' asked Gwen.

'My back's killing me, my legs ache, and what's up with these shoes?' Kevin scowled. 'Is it too much to ask for a little support?'

Gwen turned to Ben. 'He's like a real irritable, short-tempered, crotchety old man,' she whispered.

'In other words, aside from the male pattern baldness, he's pretty much the same as always,' said Ben, smirking. He started walking towards the car. 'Come on, old man.'

Kevin hobbled along behind, muttering below his breath. His frail fingers took the keys from his pocket and struggled to fit one into the door lock of his car.

'I'll drive,' said Ben, snatching the keys away from Kevin.

'Don't even think about it,' snapped Kevin. 'You don't have a licence.'

'Grandpa Max taught me,' replied Ben. 'And it's an emergency. You're near-sighted, arthritic, your reflexes are shot . . . and what's more, you're trying to unlock a cactus.'

Kevin creaked around and squinted his eyes. Sure enough, what he had thought to be the green paintwork of his car was actually a large, spiky cactus. He groaned. Maybe driving wasn't the best idea, after all.

The three heroes climbed into the vehicle, Kevin taking several minutes to clamber into the back seat. Ben slotted the keys into the ignition and the engine roared into life.

'You should have gone out with me when I was young and handsome,' Kevin told Gwen.

'You were too immature,' Gwen replied.

Kevin's eyes lit up, hopefully. 'What about now?'

'Too old.'

Before Kevin could respond, Ben floored the accelerator. The car lurched backwards and slammed into a large, metal, rubbish bin.

'Whoops!'

'It's not a bumper car,' Kevin snarled.

Up ahead, the front of a building exploded into dust. The blue creature snaked out from inside. It sped forwards, racing straight towards the car.

'Back up, back up!' cried Gwen.

Ben didn't need to be told twice. He pushed down hard on the accelerator pedal and the car launched into reverse again. His knuckles were white as he gripped on to the wheel, struggling to keep the car from spinning out of control.

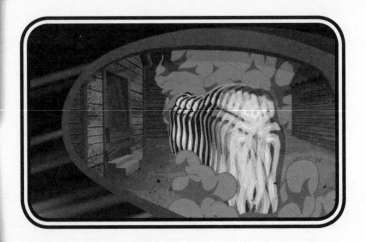

Glancing in the rear-view mirror, Ben could see that the creature was hurtling towards them. Slamming on the brakes and twisting the wheel, he sent the car into a slide. As the creature drew closer, Ben hit the gas again. The car lunged forwards into the mouth of a narrow alleyway, spewing up clouds of dust in its wake.

The ruins of the base's many buildings whizzed by on either side as Ben powered the car along the alley. He had his foot pressed hard against the floor, but it wasn't enough. The blue shape in the rear-view mirror was growing larger by the second.

And suddenly it was upon them. The creature's blue glow barely brushed against the outside of the car, but the effects were instant. The shiny green metal became brown and pitted with rust. Thick plumes of black smoke began to billow from the exhaust. Even the leather interior became worn and ripped.

'No, not the car,' wailed Kevin. 'Please, not the car!'

Even aged as it was, though, the spluttering engine still had some power left in it. The car erupted from the alleyway and skidded sharply to the right. A mound of old timber rested against a wall, forming a slope just a few hundred metres ahead. Ben steered towards it. If he could hit it just right . . .

'Hold on,' he cried, as the car sped towards the incline. He pushed even harder on the accelerator and closed his eyes, not daring to look. The car hit the makeshift ramp and launched into the air.

For a moment the three occupants of the vehicle felt weightless, before the car's tyres slammed down on to the flat roof of the building. The brakes squealed angrily as Ben kicked down on them. The car slid sideways for a few seconds, before coming to a rest right next to the edge of the roof.

They sat in silence for a few moments, waiting for their racing hearts to slow down. At last they slowly and carefully clambered out on to the roof.

'You are never driving my car again,' scowled Kevin.

'Where have you been? You were supposed to get here six seconds ago,' scolded the doctor. He was standing beside them on the rooftop, examining an old silver pocket-watch. 'Or is this thing running fast?'

'Who are you anyway?' quizzed Ben.

'What are you doing here?'

'What is that creature?' added Gwen.

'And can you fix my car?' Kevin asked.

The doctor looked at Kevin and stroked his chin, thoughtfully. 'There's something different. Is it your hair?'

'Yeah, I'm parting it down the middle now,' Kevin growled. 'And I also got real old.'

'Please don't talk to me about old,' smiled the scientist. 'I walk in eternity.'

'Well you'd better start running in eternity, smart guy!'

'Hmm, you might slow us down. I need to fix that,' the doctor said, almost to himself. He gestured with a thumb to another corner of the roof. 'We'll come back right over there.'

Gwen and Ben turned and were amazed to see the doctor standing at the other end of the roof. Kevin was beside him, young and fit once again. Ben looked around, but the old man version of Kevin was nowhere to be seen.

Gwen hurried over and threw her arms around him. 'Kevin, I can't believe it!' she beamed. 'You're good as new!'

'Well, my back still hurts a little,' Kevin said. He rested his cheek against the top of Gwen's head. 'If I could just lean on you . . .'

Gwen stepped back and gave him a playful shove. Kevin smiled, then turned to face the doctor. 'All right, professor,' he said. 'If you wouldn't mind fixing my car.'

The doctor raised an eyebrow. 'How exactly do you expect me to do that? I'm a time traveller, not a mechanic. Regressing a car would break all the Chronal laws of space–time.'

'OK, enough,' snapped Ben. The way the doctor spoke was starting to make his head ache. 'I want answers. Now.'

'Same old Ben Tennyson,' said the doctor, smiling. 'You're even more like yourself now than you were in the future.'

Kevin shook his head and sighed. 'You want me to deal with him?'

'What can you tell us, Dr Paradox?' asked Gwen.

The scientist's eyes sparkled. 'Paradox. Oh yes, that'll do. That'll do very nicely. I'll tell you a story in a way you can understand, with a beginning, middle and end.' He smiled playfully and held out his watch. A blue glow rippled across its surface. 'We'll start in the middle.'

CHAPTER FOUR

A GLIMPSE OF THE FUTURE

With a blinding flash, the three friends found themselves seeing the events of fifty years ago through Paradox's eyes. They were suddenly inside the lab, working on the big circular object they'd discovered earlier. Another scientist stood nearby, nervously studying the readings on a control panel.

'Las Solardad was built entirely because of my ingenious theory,' the doctor's voice told them. 'A time tunnel utilising the properties I discovered in quartz crystals, which would allow us access to past and future events.'

An electric-blue light began to swirl inside the machine. Ben, Gwen and Kevin could actually feel the wind as it whipped up and scattered paper and notes across the lab.

'Yeah, well for a genius, looks like you blew it,' noted Kevin.

'You don't know the half of it,' replied Paradox, grimly. 'Some tiny miscalculation on my part destabilised the experiment and ripped a hole in the fabric of reality.'

The heroes almost cried out in fright as, through the doctor's eyes, they saw the swirling portal opening up to swallow them.

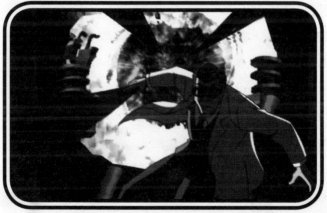

'I was hurled into the event horizon,' continued Paradox. 'I must have spent one hundred thousand years there. I didn't age or need to sleep or eat. I just existed.'

All around them, Ben and the others saw nothing but wide empty space stretching out in every direction.

'Heh. It must've been pretty boring,' Kevin said.

'At first I went quite mad, of course,' explained Paradox. 'But after a few millennia I got bored with that, too, and went sane. Very sane. I began to learn.'

With a flicker of light, Ben, Gwen and Kevin emerged from the flashback. They were back on the roof again, their legs shaking slightly from what they'd just experienced.

'I now have a total understanding of the space–time continuum,' Paradox told them. 'Allowing me to travel anywhere and in any time I want. Within reason.'

'And so where's your time machine?' asked Kevin.

'He doesn't have a time machine,' said Ben. 'He has a map in his head.'

'Exactly!' laughed the doctor. 'I know where all the shortcuts are. I spent a dozen lifetimes criss-crossing the time stream. Making it a better place.'

Kevin sneered. 'And how does that pay?'

'At the moment?' sighed Paradox. 'Not even in job satisfaction.'

The world seemed to go dim for just a fraction of a second, and all four of them were suddenly standing back in the ruins of the laboratory.

'You see, I recently discovered that some kind of extraterrestrial creature is going to wreak havoc across the universe.'

Ben frowned. 'So? The way you talk, you take on monsters like this all the time. Why's this one so bad?'

Snatching up a piece of chalk, Paradox began drawing a complicated series of scribbles on a blackboard. 'Because unlike the thousands of foes I've faced before, this extra-dimensional creature came into our plane of reality the moment my experiment went awry.'

'OK, so just to be clear,' said Kevin. 'It's your fault.'

'This creature hasn't been lurking around here for fifty years,' Gwen pointed out. 'We would know about it.'

'Time is like a river,' explained Paradox, chalking up a wavy line on the board. 'It moves, flows and bends. Fifty years ago, I accidentally set off a depth charge in that river. The creature I released was blasted fifty years in time to your present.' He scribbled all over the line on the board, wiping it out. 'Doing this to your future.'

'But all it's doing is messing up an old army base,' said Gwen. 'Why is that a problem at all? Why not just leave it alone?'

'That's a better question for the man on the moon,' chuckled Paradox.

'What?' asked Ben, confused. 'Who's the man on the moon?'

'I am,' grinned the doctor. He gestured around them at the barren, grey landscape, and twinkling stars.

Ben looked down at the dusty rocks beneath his feet. 'We're on the moon,' he said, matter-of-factly.

'No,' corrected Paradox. 'We're on the moon in your distant future.'

'What?' spluttered Kevin. 'How are we not suffocating?'

'Good question. Not remotely the point, though,' Paradox smirked. 'Imagine what the Earth would look like in two hundred years, say. With that time monster wandering all over it, aging everything that crossed its path.' He glanced at Kevin. 'For those of you with no imagination, the Earth is up there.'

They all looked up. Above their heads, a decayed planet orbited silently through space.

'You've brought us to the worst possible version of the future,' said Ben.

'No. Should I fail to stop that creature, this is your best possible future.' He waited a moment, letting his words sink in. 'Not a pretty sight, is it?'

A figure suddenly appeared a few metres ahead of them. It stood with its back to the group, gazing up at the shrivelled Earth.

'What are you doing here?' asked Paradox.

The newcomer turned around. It was the doctor. Or an identical version of him, at least. Kevin shook his head. This was frying his brain.

'I'm allowing myself to feel the full

impact of my failure,' replied the other Paradox.

'OK,' sighed Kevin. 'Who's he?'

'He's a parallel Paradox,' Ben guessed.

'Young Ben has an innate sense of trans-temporal metaphysics,' the new doctor smiled. 'It will serve him well in his past.'

Ben grinned, pleased by the compliment, even if he didn't really understand it. 'And I drive good, too,' he added.

Kevin suddenly remembered the rusted old vehicle back on Earth. 'We can breathe on the moon in the future, but you can't fix my car?' he scowled.

'What should I do?' asked the first Paradox, ignoring him.

'Well, obviously not what I did,' shrugged the other. 'But whatever you do, you better do it quickly.' He turned his gaze back up to the lifeless husk of the planet Earth. 'Time is running out!'

CHAPTER FIVE

SOLVING THE MYSTERY

Reality flickered around them, and Ben, Gwen and Kevin found themselves back in the abandoned army base. Paradox was with them. Thankfully there was only one of him.

'So why do we come back here? Why don't we just travel back in time and stop the time experiment from ever happening?' suggested Gwen.

'Isn't that just like an energy being to think outside temporal conventions?' chuckled Paradox. 'The experiment that releases the creature also unsticks me in time. And that must happen, because, uh, in all modesty . . .'

'You've saved the world dozens of times,' concluded Ben.

'Hundreds, actually. In fact, on one

occasion you and I worked together to save the entire uni . . .' His voice trailed off and he shook his head. 'Never mind. It should be here any – '

KRAAK-OOOM!

The deafening roar of an explosion tore through the base. Paradox nodded. 'You could set your watch by it.'

Ben was setting his watch, but not in the way Paradox had meant. He adjusted the Omnitrix and scrolled through four or five of his alien forms. At last he found the one he was looking for.

'Jet Ray!' he cried, transforming into the red, winged alien. He launched himself into the air in time to see the blue creature emerge from one of the derelict buildings.

Jet Ray rained down a torrent of energy blasts on the monster. Each blast merely passed through the thing, not damaging it at all.

Paradox grabbed a handful of gumballs from the bag in his pocket. He hurled them at the ground just in front of the creature. It slipped and skidded a couple of times on the hard balls of coloured candy, then stopped.

'They hit it?' asked a puzzled Jet Ray, touching down next to the group. 'Doesn't everything age into oblivion as soon as they touch it?'

'Gumballs last a really long time. Look under your desk at school,' Paradox replied. His eyes went wide with fright. 'Now get back!'

Jet Ray turned to see the creature speeding towards him. He kicked out with his powerful legs and flew out of its path at the very last moment.

Gwen raised her hands. Energy crackled across her fingertips, but before she could unleash an attack, Paradox threw himself into the creature's path. He caught hold of it and pushed, bravely trying to force it back.

'Let go,' Gwen cried. 'Or he'll age you into dust!'

'I exist outside of time,' replied Paradox through gritted teeth. 'But I can still feel the eons passing.'

Realising he was useless in his current form, Jet Ray flew down to land and changed back into Ben.

'Paradox, take us back to the accident,' he barked. 'Now!'

The doctor grunted. The effort of holding the creature back was draining all his strength. 'But I told you – '

'Just do it!'

One brief, blinding flash later, the heroes and the time-creature all found themselves back in 1955. Around them stood the same army base, only now it looked brand new.

'Kevin, Gwen, the lab, quick,' ordered Ben. He turned to Paradox. 'You just keep that thing occupied.'

'Keep . . . keep it occupied?' echoed the doctor. 'I'm a time-travelling hero. I don't keep things occupied!'

The door to the lab opened quietly, and Ben, Gwen and Kevin snuck inside. An imposing army general stood in front of a window, watching the experiment that was soon to take place on the other side of the glass.

'Sure this thing is gonna work?' the general barked into the handset of a telephone. 'Your time machine has cost the US government a pretty penny, doctor.'

Unseen by anyone, the three heroes crept out of the observation booth and into the main part of the lab. They crawled along the floor below the window, their eyes scanning the room for anything that might tell them how to stop the strange creature.

'As to cost,' said the doctor, continuing his conversation with the general, 'I would say that the alleviation of untold human suffering throughout history is ample justification.'

Down on the floor, a thought suddenly occurred to Ben. 'Why would it use the phone?' he whispered.

Gwen frowned. 'What?'

'The creature. It tried to use the payphone. Then it went to the police station. Then the dorms. It didn't act like some unfathomable trans-dimensional creature. It did everything a normal person would do.'

Gwen nodded, finally understanding. 'If they suddenly found themselves in an abandoned military base.'

With a roar, a wind whipped up around them. The doctor had thrown the switch to start the machine!

They looked up in time to see Hugo, the lab assistant, accidentally knocking a heavy tool box on to a control panel. The machinery fizzled and spat as the circuitry inside went haywire.

The wind in the lab immediately increased in strength. Electricity buzzed across the surface of the time machine. The doctor stumbled forwards, and then he was tumbling across the lab. He cried out in terror as he was swallowed up by the swirling energy of the Chronologger.

'Help!' yelped another voice. Hugo was clinging tightly to a metal pole. His legs were dragged out behind him, toes pointing towards the machine. His knuckles were white. He couldn't hold on much longer.

Ben leapt up and stretched out a hand.

As he did, he felt his own feet begin to slip on the rough concrete floor.

'You'll get sucked in along with him!' Gwen shrieked.

'I need to put on a little weight,' Ben realised. He slapped his hand down on to the Omnitrix and felt the energy swirling around him. The room shook as he stretched and grew into the hulking, dinosaur-like Humungousaur.

Shocked by the sudden appearance of the monstrous alien, Hugo let his fingers slip from the pole. For a split-second he was hurtling towards the Chronologger, before something brought him to an abrupt stop.

Hugo looked up to see an enormous hand gripping his arm. Humungousaur's mouth curved into a smile, revealing two rows of worryingly sharp teeth.

'Trust me,' said the dino-alien, 'this beats the alternative.'

With a grunt, Humungousaur pulled Hugo free of the swirling whirlwind. Energy flared at Gwen's fingertips, then crackled across the room. In a flash of purple, the time machine exploded, showering the lab with shards of stone and hot metal.

Outside the lab, Paradox wrestled with the time-creature. He was growing weaker. Any second now his legs would give way and the monster would be free to rampage across the whole globe.

And then, without warning, the creature stopped fighting. Paradox looked down to see the semi-conscious form of his old assistant,

Hugo, where the monster had been.

'Hugo,' he said with a gasp. Suddenly it all made perfect sense. 'Of course. If it were a snake it would have bit me.'

At the sound of their footsteps, Paradox turned to find Ben, Gwen and Kevin approaching. 'Well, don't look so smug,' he told them. 'I would have figured it out eventually.'

'You had a hundred thousand years,' Ben reminded him.

Paradox smiled. He released Hugo, who was slowly coming round, then stepped over to join his fellow heroes. In a flash of blue all four of them vanished, leaving behind one very confused lab assistant.

Back in the present, Paradox was preparing to say his goodbyes.

'Well, I have to admit it, I'm impressed,' he said. 'All those centuries trapped in the event horizon and it never occurred to me that the accident wasn't my fault.' He smiled at Ben. 'You're much smarter than you were when I met you years later.'

As Ben tried to figure out if that was a compliment or not, Gwen stepped forwards. 'And so what happened to him?' she asked. 'Your lab assistant?'

'I lived my life,' spoke a hoarse voice from behind her.

They all turned to see Hugo shuffling up to join them. He looked older than he'd looked when they'd last seen him. Fifty years older.

'Hugo,' beamed Paradox. 'How are you?'

'I'm well, and you look the same,' Hugo replied. 'And I haven't seen you in fifty years.'

'Well, I haven't seen you in a hundred thousand years,' Paradox told him. 'And you don't look that bad. How was your life?'

'Good,' Hugo nodded. 'A good life. But, I'm . . . I'm sorry about the experiment. I ruined everything. I never got to time travel.'

Paradox raised an eyebrow. 'Would you still like to?'

'Yes. I'm not afraid any more.'

'Glad to hear it!' He put his arm around Hugo and began to lead him towards a swirling blue portal that had appeared just a few metres away. 'How about I give you a behind-the-scenes look at eternity?'

And with that, the two old friends

stepped into the time portal, and vanished.

'Well, at least he's got company now,' said Gwen. 'He won't be lonely any more.'

'Oh, and thanks for stranding us out here in the middle of nowhere,' Kevin shouted, even though Paradox wasn't around to hear him.

'Come on,' shrugged Ben. 'We've got a long walk home.'

The three of them trudged off towards one of the holes in the base's security wall. As they turned the first corner, Kevin's eyes went wide with wonder. His car sat in the middle of the road, its green paintwork gleaming.

'It looks like new,' gasped Gwen.

'It doesn't just look like new,' Kevin laughed. 'It's factory new from thirty years ago. Paradox, I take back everything I was about to say about you.'

A scrap of paper under one of the windscreen wipers caught Ben's eye. He picked it up, unfolded it and began to read.

'Kevin,' he read, 'try to keep in mind that if this car comes into contact with anything else from 1976, it will explode like anti-matter. Enjoy! Paradox.'

Ben folded the note and passed it to Kevin. 'He's kidding, right?' asked Kevin, the smile fading from his face.

Gwen and Ben climbed into the car, grinning to themselves.

'That's some kind of time-travel joke, right?' Kevin fretted. 'Isn't it? Guys?'

On the back seat, Ben gazed out at the army base. They had done it again. They had saved the world. And even though he may be a little strange, it was nice to know that someday, somehow, they would cross paths with Paradox again.